Ready Set Go Books, an Open Hearts Big Dreams Project

Learn more about
Ready Set Go Books

http://openheartsbigdreams.org/book-project/

Ready Set Read Stories
from Ethiopia
Volume 1

First Stories
for Reading Practice

Reading has the power to change lives

but many children and adults in Ethiopia cannot read. One reason is that Ethiopia has very few easy-to-read books in local languages to give children and adults a chance to practice reading. Ready Set Go books wants to close that gap and open a world of ideas and possibilities for these kids and their communities. When you buy a Ready Set Go book, you provide critical funding to create and distribute more books.

Two Ethiopian girls reading the first book
they have seen in their own language

These three book were inspired by wise sayings from Ethiopia. Ethiopian conversation is full of proverbs and fables and wise sayings that many people know and use. The wise sayings often rhyme in Amharic. If an adult says the first half, many children can chant the second half. Sometimes the meaning of these sayings is clear. Sometimes it has to be puzzled out and argued over. But sayings, idioms, and proverbs help people express truths and beliefs in unusual ways.

Fifty Lemons

ሃምሳ ሎሚ

English and Amharic

One lemon.

አንድ ሎሚ።

Ten lemons.

አስር ሎሚ።

Twenty lemons.

ሃያ ሎሚ።

Fifty lemons make a
heavy load.

ሃምሳ ሎሚ ለአንድ
ሰው ከባድ ሸክም ነው።

The stream is deep.

ምንጩ ጥልቀት
ያለው ነው።

The road is steep.

መንገዱ
ቁልቁለታማ ነው።

The smell is strong.

ሽታው ያውዳል።

The hill is long.

አቅበቱ ረኺም ነው።

ልጁም መንገድ ዳር
ተከዞ ቆሟል።

The boy stands sadly
by the road.

One friend.

እንድ ጓደኛ።

Ten friends.

አስር ጓደኞች ።

Twenty friends.

ሃያ ጓደኞች።

Fifty friends all take one.

ሃምሳ ጓደኞች ሁሉም
እንዳንድ ወሰዱ።

For one person,
fifty lemons
is a heavy load.

ሃምሳ ሎሚ ለአንድ
ሰው ሸክሙ ነው፡፡

For fifty people, fifty lemons
are gems for the road!

ሃምሳ ሎሚ ለአንድ ሰው
ሸክሙ ለሃምሳ ሰው ጌጡ!

Behind The Story

One of our consultants, Woubeshet Ayenew, who is also a cardiologist in Minneapolis, Minnesota, volunteers to help make translations of Ready Set Go books both accurate and appealing to young readers. Woubeshet translated this saying like this:

For one person, fifty lemons is a heavy load.
For fifty people, fifty lemons are adornments.

We used a simpler English word for our story to help with reading practice.

Woubeshet says that in his home region of Ethiopia, people stand on the bridge over the Blue Nile River, make a wish, and then toss a lomi (lemon) into the river to make their wish come true. In that region, the lomi is yellow. The river is afloat with yellow dots! In other regions, lomis are green and look like what we call a "lime" in the United States.

24

Illustrators

Two students--Ruby Stott and Eden Hakala--and one adult, Jackie Farah, started illustration for this book. Ruby Stott was 11 years old and a 5th grade student at Montessori School of Beaverton in Portland, Oregon, when she created most of the illustrations for this book.

She has a keen interest in cooking, travel and art. She enjoys anything creative, playing soccer with her friends and reading.

Ruby working on "Fifty Lemons" art

Jackie and Eden with a few books and lemons for inspiration

We Can Stop
the Lion

ድር ቢያብር

English and Amharic

28

One spider dances.

አንድ ሸረሪት ትደንሳለች።

The lion sleeps.

አንበሳው ተኝቷል።

30

Two spiders dance.

ሁለት ሸረሪቶች
ይደንሳሉ።

The lion sleeps.

አንበሳው አሁንም
ተኝቷል።

Three spiders dance.

ሦስት ሸረሪቶች
ይደንሳሉ።

The lion wakes up!

አንበሳው ተነሳ!

UH-OH!

አቤት-አቤት!

The lion stretches.

አንበሳው ተንጠራራ።

The lion growls!

አንበሳው አጉረመረመ!

One spider spins.

አንድ ሸረሪት ድሮን አጠነጠነችበት፡፡

Two spiders spin.

ሁለት ሸረሪቶች
ድራቸውን አጠነጠኑበት።

Three spiders spin.

ሦስት ሸረሪቶች
ድራቻውን አጠነጠኑበት።

Ah-ha!

አሃ!

When spiders
work together,
they can stop a lion!

ድር ቢያብር
አንበሳ ያስር!

Behind The Story

Lions have been an important symbol for Ethiopia. During the reign of the emperor Haile Selassie, for example, the royal flag showed a crowned lion carrying a cross. Today, lion populations across much of Africa are considered vulnerable, so in 2016 wildlife conservationists from Oxford University in England were happy to confirm stories from park staff of lions living in the Alatash National Park in Northwest Ethiopia, close to the Sudan border.

A sculpture of the crowned Lion of Judah in the Ethiopian National Museum

This boy at an Ethiopia Read library knew to have the little girl count the spiders, thanks to good modeling from the staff.

Illustrators

Two young illustrators, Humphrey Nelms and Celeste Burkholder began work on this project.
Celeste was 11 years old and a 5th grade student at Montessori School of Beaverton near Portland, Oregon, when she created most of the illustrations for this book. She likes to play soccer (football) with her friends, draw, read books, and sing.
Her favorite subjects in school are science and art.

Humphrey at work and
Celeste's finished masterpiece

Walls of Grass

የሰንበሌጥ ግድግዳዎች

English and Amharic

We need new houses.

አዳዲስ ቤቶችን መሥራት እንፈልጋለን።

Slow.

በቀስታ፤ በዝግታ።

Slow, slow.

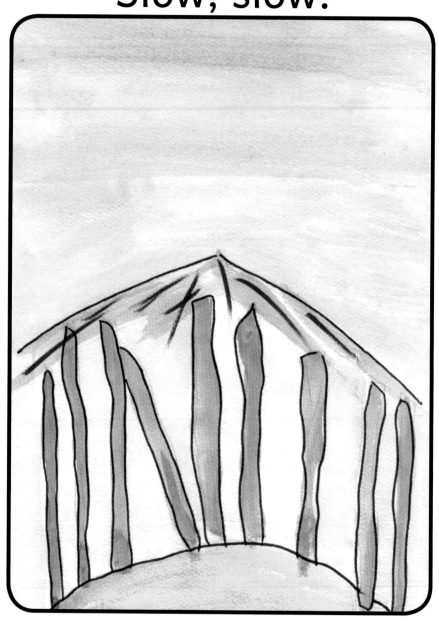

ቀስ ፤ ዝግ ብለን።

Slow, slow, slow.

አሁንም ቀስ፤ ዝግ፤ ብለን።

Finished!

አለቀ!

Is it strong?
እውነት
ቤቱ ጠንካራ ነው?

How long will it last?

ምን ያህል ይቆያል?

One day
a strong wind blows.

አንድ ቀን ኃይለኛ ንፋስ
ነፈሰ።

It is strong. It will last.

ምንም ንቅንቅ አላለም።
ያለምንም ችግር ለረጅም
ጊዜ ይቆያል።

That was too slow.

ያ ግን በጣም ቀስ፤ ዝግ
ያለ አሠራር ነበር።

Let's work fast.

አሁን በፍጥነት፤ ቶሎ
ቶሎ እንሥራ።

Fast!

ቶሎ፤ ቶሎ!

Fast, fast!

በፍጥነት፤ ቶሎ ቶሎ!

Fast, fast, fast!

አሁንም በፍጥነት፤ ቶሎ
ቶሎ፤ ቶሎ ቶሎ! 63

Finished!

አለቀ!

Is the house strong?

እውነት ቤቱ ጠንካራ ነው?

How long will it last?

ምን ያህል ይቆያል?

One day a strong wind blows.

አንድ ቀን ኃይለኛ ንፋስ ነፈሰ።

Oh no!

አዬ... ጉድ!

Things made fast never last!

የእነቶሎ ቶሎ
ቤት ግድግዳው
ሰንበለጥ!

Behind The Story

Houses in Ethiopia can be big and modern or small and traditional. The walls can be made from concrete or stones. In cities and towns, they usually have a rectangular shape. But most houses in the countryside have round walls made from a clay dirt mixed with straw to make a strong, adobe-like material. Roofs for those houses are made from thatch that is usually cut at the end of the rainy season.

Word-for-word the Ethiopian saying might translate this way:

The fast-fast house--walls of thatch.

A traditional house or tukle with some extra flare.

Illustrator

Beth Neel is an amateur artist who loves trying things out. Her inspiration for some of the illustrations came from traditional Ethiopian icons of angels and saints and stories from the Bible. Illustrating the Ready Set Go books has been a joy!

This teacher had never shared a book in his own language before these books were delivered to this WEEMA kindergarten.

Translation is currently being coordinated by a new volunteer, Amlaku Bikss Eshetie who has a BA degree in Foreign Languages & Literature, an MA in Teaching English as a Foreign Language, and PhD courses in Applied Linguistics and Communication, all at Addis Ababa University. He taught English from elementary through university levels and is currently a passionate and experienced English-Amharic translator. His connections to translators for Tigrinya and Afaan Oromo have made this project possible. As a father of three, he also has a special interest in child literacy and development.

He can be reached at: khaabba_ils@protonmail.com

Amharic is a Semitic language—in fact, the world's second-most widely spoken Semitic language (with Arabic being the first). Starting in the 12th century, it became the Ethiopian language that was used in official transactions and schools and became widely spoken all over Ethiopia. It's written with its own characters, over 260 of them. Eritrea and Ethiopia share this alphabet, and they are the only countries in Africa to develop a writing system centuries ago that is still in use today.

Thank you to the generous team who gave
their time and talents to make
this book possible.

Writer
Jane Kurtz

Creative Directors
Jane Kurtz and Caroline Kurtz

Designers
Kenny and Ashley Rasmussen

Translators
Amlaku B. Eshetie
Woubeshet Ayenew

Special thanks to Ethiopia Reads donors and staff
for believing in this project and helping get it
started-- and for currently coordinating professional
development opportunities and distribution in
Ethiopia.

Illustrations for these three stories grew out of a
bookmaking workshop at Westminster Presbyterian
Church in Portland, OR.

Nonprofit Collaboration at Its Best

Ethiopia Reads was started by volunteers in places like Grand Forks, North Dakota; Denver, Colorado; San Francisco, California; and Washington D.C. who wanted to give the gift of reading to more kids in Ethiopia.

One of the founders, Jane Kurtz, learned to read in Ethiopia where she spent most of her childhood and where the circle of life has come around to bring her Ethiopian-American grandchildren. As a children's book author, Jane is the driving force behind Ready Set Go Books – working to create the books that inspire those just learning to read.

Open Hearts Big Dreams began as a volunteer organization, led by Ellenore Angelidis in Seattle, Washington, to provide sustainable funding and strategic support to Ethiopia Reads, collaborating with Jane Kurtz. OHBD has now grown to be its own nonprofit organization supporting literacy, art, and technology for young people in Ethiopia.

Ellenore Angelidis comes from a family of teachers who believe education is a human right, and opportunity should not depend on your birthplace. And as the adoptive mother of a little girl who was born in Ethiopia and learned to read in the US, as well as an aspiring author, she finds the chance to positively impact literacy hugely compelling.

Made in the USA
Middletown, DE
29 January 2019